26/8/22

D1685704

ROY

Please renew or return items by the date shown on your receipt

www.hertfordshire.gov.uk/libraries

Renewals and enquiries: 0300 123 4049

Textphone for hearing or 0300 123 4041
speech impaired users:

L32 11.16

526 154 83 1

With special thanks to Anne Marie Ryan

ORCHARD BOOKS
Carmelite House
50 Victoria Embankment
London EC4Y 0DZ

This edition published by Orchard Books in 2017

A CIP catalogue record for this book is available
from the British Library.

ISBN 978 1 40834 638 9

1 3 5 7 9 10 8 6 4 2

Printed in China

Orchard Books
An imprint of Hachette Children's Group
Part of The Watts Publishing Group Limited
An Hachette UK Company
www.hachette.co.uk

SIDESWIPE'S BRAVE PLAN

ORCHARD

ROLL OUT!

BUMBLEBEE

SIDESWIPE

STRONGARM

GRIMLOCK

FIXIT

CONTENTS

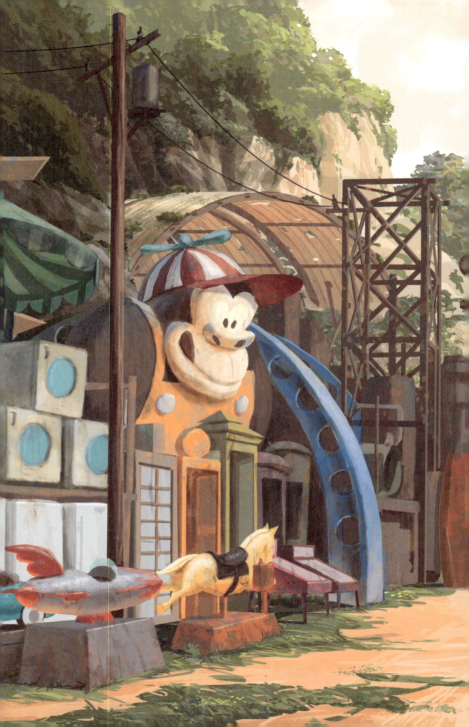

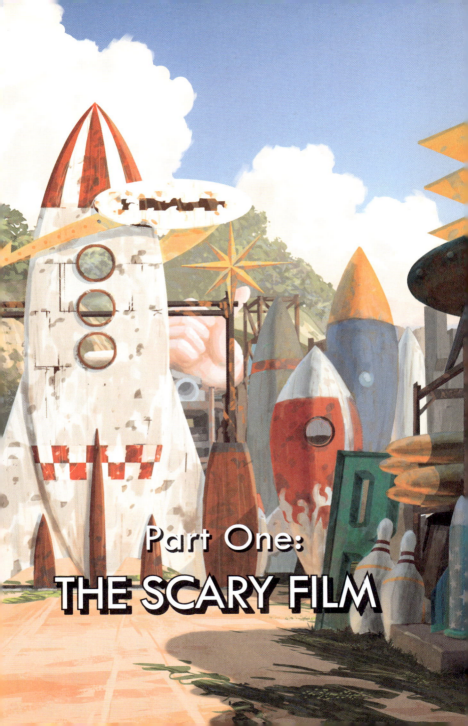

Part One:
THE SCARY FILM

Chapter One

HOME ALONE

It was Friday night and Russell Clay had finished school.
His dad was going out with Bumblebee and Fixit.

"Will you be OK on your own?" Denny asked Russell.

"Of course I will," said Russell. "But I won't be on my own." His robot friends Sideswipe, Strongarm and Grimlock were all there too.

"You should watch a fun …
I mean, a film," Fixit said. The
little robot sometimes got his
words muddled up!

"Yes," said Russell. "I'm going
to watch a scary film about a
zombie attack!"

"Won't you be scared?"
asked Denny, sounding worried.

"Of course not. I'm not scared
of anything!" boasted Russell.

Denny laughed. Russell was a
very brave boy. Denny waved
goodbye and they left.

Sideswipe was a big red robot. He had heard what Russell had said to his dad. Sideswipe was tough and liked to show off. But he had a secret – sometimes he felt scared!

Sideswipe sighed. "That kid's not afraid of anything," he said to Grimlock.

"I'm not afraid of anything either," growled Grimlock. Grimlock was a huge robot who could turn into a dinobot.

Just then, a cute little kitten padded up to the two robots.

"Meow!" said the kitten.

"Aarrggghh!" screamed the big dinobot, running away.

Grimlock *was* scared of something. He was scared of kittens!

Chapter Two

SHOW TIME

Russell sat down on the sofa in front of the television. He had a big bowl of popcorn. "This is going to be awesome," he said, switching on the film.

Sideswipe, Strongarm and Grimlock gathered around the window so they could watch the film too.

Sideswipe shivered nervously as spooky music began to play.

On the TV screen, zombies were chasing the hero down the street. There was lots of screaming.

Russell just laughed and ate his popcorn.

Sideswipe didn't like the film.

He felt scared. But he didn't say anything because he didn't want his friends to tease him.

Sideswipe peeked at the TV screen. Now the zombies had the hero trapped in a small room. There was no way out!

Sideswipe hated being trapped. He covered his eyes and screamed.

"You're a scaredy-cat, Sideswipe," said Grimlock.

"At least I'm not scared of cats," said Sideswipe.

"Ha ha!" laughed Strongarm.

"Good one, Sideswipe."

Russell tossed the last piece of popcorn in his mouth. "Well, I'm not scared of ANYTHING," he said, stopping the film and going to get more popcorn.

"I don't believe him," said Sideswipe. "Everybody's scared of SOMETHING."

"Well, there's only one way to find out," said Strongarm.

"What do you mean, Strongarm?" asked Grimlock.

"I bet we can scare Russell!" Strongarm said, her blue eyes flashing with excitement.

Chapter Three

ZOMBIE ATTACK

When Russell came back with a new bowlful of popcorn, all the Autobots were gone. "Hey! Where is everyone?" he called.

"RAAARH!" Sideswipe jumped out at him. He was pretending to be a zombie! Sideswipe had put a mop on his head as a disguise. He stuck out his arms and walked stiffly across the scrapyard.

"I'm coming to get you, Russell," he growled.

But Russell wasn't fooled. "Nice try, Sideswipe," he said. "Now, come here or you'll miss the rest of the film."

Sideswipe sighed and took off the mop.

But before Russell could switch the film back on, a voice called, "Help! I've been attacked by a Decepticon!" It was Strongarm!

Russell gasped and ran to her.

Strongarm was lying on the floor. "The Decepticon got me," she said weakly. "And he's right behind you!"

Grimlock rose up tall and roared. He was pretending to be a Decepticon — a bad robot.

Sideswipe jumped. He thought the dinobot looked very scary. Grimlock roared again.

Russell just laughed. "Face it, everyone," he said, grinning. "I can't be scared!"

"Everybody!" Denny called as he, Fixit and Bumblebee arrived back at the scrapyard. Fixit's scanner was beeping. They all crowded around the screen.

"I am detecting an enemy in the caves," said Fixit.

There was a real Decepticon on the loose! This was no time for fun. It was time for action. They had to find it!

Part Two:
DANGER IN THE CAVES

Chapter Four

SEARCH PARTY

The Autobots turned into cars and sped to the caves. Denny and Russell went with Sideswipe, who had changed into a fast red race car.

"The caves are too big to search as a group," said Bumblebee when they got there. "We'll need to split up."

"I know these caves pretty well," said Denny. "Count me in."

"Thanks," said Bumblebee. "Fixit, you and Russell can both stay out here."

"Why can't I go in?" moaned Russell. "I'm not scared of going in the caves!"

"I need you to look after Fixit," explained Bumblebee.

Russell was annoyed. He wanted to go in the caves too!

Sideswipe wished he could stay outside!

"Here's some glow-in-the-dark paint," said Denny. He gave each of the Autobots a paintbrush and some paint. "Leave some paint behind as you go so that you don't get lost," he told them.

Grimlock couldn't wait to get started. "Let's go!" he said.

Denny and the Autobots went into the cave. They each headed a different way. Every few steps they painted a mark on the wall.

The caves were dark and spooky. There were lots of tunnels and they all looked the same. Before long, Denny was completely lost.

Sideswipe was searching a long, dark tunnel nearby.

He felt scared but knew he had to be brave. Suddenly, he heard a loud shrieking sound. Sideswipe turned and gasped. A bad robot with wings like a bat was flying right at him. It was a Decepticon!

Chapter Five

AUTOBOTS UNDER ATTACK!

"Sideswipe, come in!" Bumblebee called through his radio. But there was no reply. "Has anyone heard from Sideswipe?" Bumblebee asked.

Outside, Russell and Fixit were looking at a screen. On the screen there were pictures showing where all the robots were.

BLEEP!

Sideswipe's picture flashed and then it was gone.

"Oh, no! We've lost Sideswipe," said Fixit.

Then Grimlock's picture vanished too.

"What's going on in there?" asked Russell.

Then Strongarm's picture disappeared.

"We're losing them all," cried Fixit. The little robot was upset.

Russell tried to warn the others. "Bumblebee! Dad! Get out of there fast!" he called.

Bumblebee ran through the caves looking for the rest of his team. His sword glowed as he searched a tunnel. He felt very worried. He could not find the other Autobots.

Bumblebee suddenly heard a horrible, loud shrieking noise. Then the Decepticon attacked him! It grabbed Bumblebee and flew off.

Outside the cave, Russell and Fixit stared at the screen.

Bumblebee's picture had disappeared. Now the whole team was gone!

Russell and Fixit looked at each other. Russell gulped. "I'm sure everyone's OK," he said bravely.

Chapter Six

NIGHTSTRIKE APPEARS

Russell's dad, Denny, wandered through the caves. He was still lost. He saw one of the glow-in-the-dark marks he'd painted. Then he saw another one.

"Oh, no," said Denny. "I must be going around in circles!"

Outside, Fixit was very worried about the Autobots. "What if they fell into a pit of hot lava?" he said anxiously.

"Or what if they were eaten by rock monsters?"

"Calm down," Russell told the robot. "The rocks are probably blocking the signals."

A loud shriek came from inside the cave. The bat-like Decepticon flew out, flapping its huge wings. Fixit was so scared he shut his eyes tight.

"Pull yourself together," Russell told Fixit. "Look that thing up on your computer. Quickly, before it comes back!"

Fixit looked on his computer.

"He's called Nightstrike," said Fixit. "His screams make you have bad dreams."

"What a nightmare. And he's coming back!" shouted Russell.

The Decepticon shrieked and swooped down. Russell ran but Fixit was too scared to move. Nightstrike grabbed the little robot with his sharp claws.

Just then, Denny finally found his way out of the cave.

"I made it!" he cried happily.

But the Decepticon snatched him up too and flew back into the cave.

"Dad!" cried Russell. "Fixit!" But he was all alone. Russell picked up the torch his dad had dropped. "OK, guys," he said, heading into the caves. "It's Russell to the rescue!"

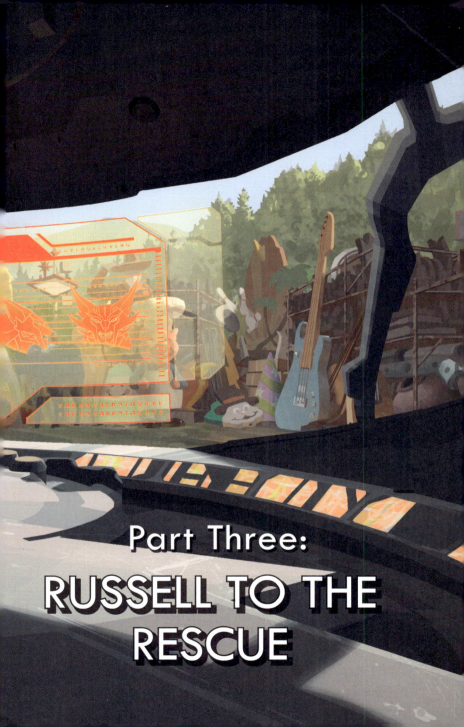

Part Three:

RUSSELL TO THE RESCUE

Chapter Seven

SCARY DREAMS

"Dad! Sideswipe! Anyone!" called Russell as he ran around the caves. His cries echoed through the empty tunnels.

Russell shone his torch around and saw a huge shadow on the wall. He gasped and tripped. It looked like a monster but it was only a little mouse!

"Maybe I DO get scared," Russell told himself, getting up.

"But I can't be scared right now!
The team needs me."

They did need him. Deep
in the caves, Nightstrike had
trapped them all and was
screaming. His screams were
giving the robots bad dreams.

Bumblebee was dreaming that Optimus Prime was telling him off and he was very sad.

"I am so disappointed in you, Bumblebee," said Optimus Prime, tapping his feet very crossly.

"I chose you to lead this mission and you have failed. You are not ready to be in charge."

"No!" cried Bumblebee. Letting his hero down was his worst fear!

Strongarm was dreaming that she was being chased by the police.

"You have the wrong robot!" she told them.

"You're under arrest," said a police officer. He put handcuffs on her. "You are a disgrace to the force."

"I'm innocent!" cried Strongarm in her sleep. The police car bot was terrified of breaking the rules.

Sideswipe was dreaming that he was stuck in a traffic jam. Cars piled up all around him.

He was trapped!

"Get me out of here!" howled Sideswipe.

And Grimlock was dreaming about a cute little kitten.

"Leave me alone!" Grimlock yelled as the kitten meowed at him. It was his worst nightmare!

Chapter Eight

BREAK OUT!

Russell spotted one of his dad's glow-in-the-dark marks. He followed the trail of paint and found his dad and the robots. Nightstrike had trapped them all in hard cocoons. Denny was struggling to break out.

"Dad!" gasped Russell.

Denny saw Russell, who was hiding behind a rock. He tried to distract the Decepticon.

"I think I heard something, over there!" he said, pointing down the tunnel. "It must be a rescue party," Denny told Nightstrike.

"Where?" Nightstrike said.

He flew off to look for intruders. When the coast was clear, Russell ran over to his dad.

"How did you find us?" Denny asked his son.

"I'll explain later," Russell told him. "Let's get you out of here."

He picked up a sharp rock and started to chip away at his dad's cocoon. Blue goo poured out. Soon Denny was free.

But just then, Nightstrike came back and saw Russell. Russell gasped as the horrible Decepticon came over to him.

"This little human is no match for me," he laughed. "I can stop him easily."

"You'll have to catch me first!" Russell said.

Chapter Nine

SIDESWIPE'S BRAVE PLAN

Russell ran away and Nightstrike chased after him, shrieking loudly. Denny grabbed a rock and started opening Bumblebee's cocoon. Sideswipe was getting free as well.

Nightstrike flew even faster. He was going to catch Russell.

Russell needed some help!

Sideswipe knew he had to be as brave as Russell. He needed to think of a plan, quick!

"Why are you wasting your time on that human?" Sideswipe called out. "You big, horrible Decepticon! Pick on someone your own size, like me!"

Nightstrike turned and glared at Sideswipe with cold green eyes. He flew at the red robot, but he missed.

Just then, Denny managed to free Bumblebee. The big yellow bot hit Nightstrike with his sword. Sparks flew through the air. The rest of the cocoons cracked open. The Autobots were all free!

Nightstrike shrieked in anger. Then Sideswipe had another good idea. "Robots!" he cried. "Turn off your sound receptors."

The sound receptors were like the robots' ears! Now the Autobots couldn't hear the Decepticon's screams. He couldn't make them have any more dreams. They charged at Nightstrike with their weapons.

Grimlock got there first. He jumped on Nightstrike and knocked him to the ground. The Autobots had saved the day!

Back at the scrapyard, they put Nightstrike in a stasis pod where he could not hurt anyone.

"You were right, Russell," said Denny. "You don't get scared."

"Are you kidding?" said Russell. "Without you and my friends I was really scared."

Denny hugged his son.

"Everyone gets scared sometimes," said Bumblebee.

"Being scared isn't a bad thing. Real bravery is doing things even when you're scared."

"I'm not afraid of anything," said Grimlock.

An adorable kitten padded up to Grimlock and purred.

"Help!" screamed the dinobot, running away in fear.

Sideswipe grinned. It was good to know that even the bravest, toughest robots sometimes got scared like him … and that was OK!

The End

WELL DONE!

You've finished this adventure!